THE FABULOUS PRINCIPAL PIE

WRITTEN BY
JAMES HOFFMAN

ILLUSTRATED BY
NAN BROOKS

The children at school
were not very pleased.
Lunch was runny hot jello
and ice cold peas.

So they all decided to
make up a meal
to let the cooks know
how they really feel.

All of a sudden Calvin stood.
"I'll give you an idea
of what foods sound good!

"How about a cup
of lollipop soup
to have with a bite
of peanut butter goop?

"Or banana dogs
and root beer pie
or bubble gum stew
with nuts piled high?

"Pies will be cherry and berry and coconut cream topped with tons and tons of chocolate ice cream.

"We'll have trucks and trains
of sugary stuff covered
with mounds and mounds
of marshmallow puffs.

"How about trays of
apple crown roast
to eat with slices of
honey brown toast?

"Let's have cheese BLT's
with watermelon first,
then ice cube jello
to crunch our thirst.

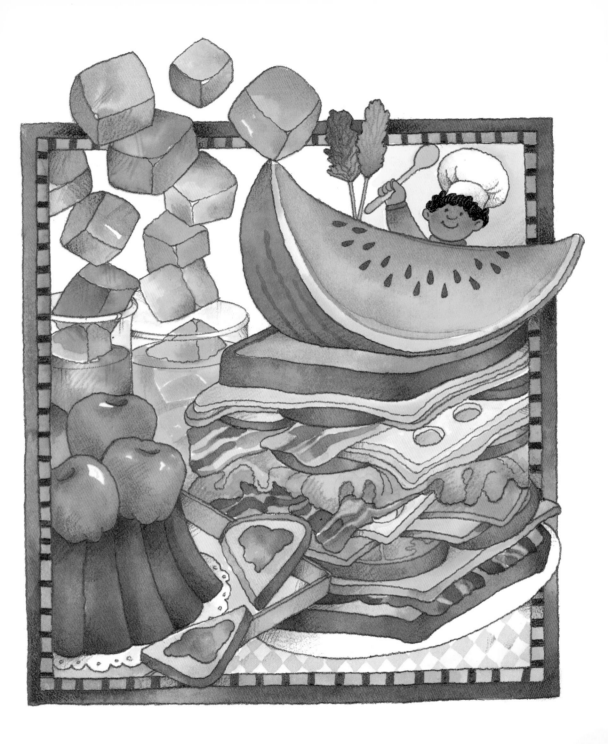

"A great big chocolate
fudge thing molded . . ."
then the principal walked in,
his arms sternly folded.

"Ah – we could also
have some Principal Pie
to show our thanks
to a very nice guy!

"A Principal Pie
that's handsome and nice
with very good fruit
and just the right spice.

"A crust that is tender
but does not fall apart,
with fruit that is sweet
and just enough tart.

"These are a few of
the reasons why
we call it the
Fabulous Principal Pie!"

The principal smiled
and gave a wink.
"Our next meal can be made
by Calvin, I think."